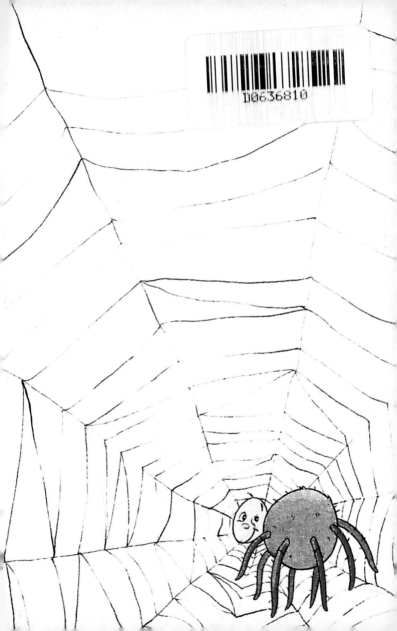

© 1994 Geddes & Grosset Ltd
Published by Geddes & Grosset Ltd,
New Lanark, Scotland.

ISBN   1 85534 569 2

Printed and bound in Slovenia.

Dame Trot and her Pig

Retold by Judy Hamilton
Illustrated by R. James Binnie

Tarantula Books

Once upon a time there was an old woman called Dame Trot, who lived in a tiny cottage all alone. One day, while she was busy sweeping the floor, she found a silver coin under a rug.

"A silver coin!" she said, " What luck! I think I shall buy a pig with this coin, to keep me company. If I hurry, I can get to market, buy the pig, and get home in time for supper."

Dame Trot set off at once and hurried to market where she bought a nice, plump, little pig. Then she hurried off homewards with the pig scurrying behind. But when they came to the stile the pig sat down. Dame Trot spoke to the pig:

"Pig, please, Pig, climb over the stile, or I shan't get home in time for supper."

But the pig would not climb over the stile.

Dame Trot looked around for some help and she saw a dog. She went up to the dog and said:

"Dog, please Dog, will you bite my pig?

Pig won't climb over the stile and I shan't get home in time for supper."

But the dog would not bite her pig.

So Dame Trot looked around for some more help and she saw a stick. She went up to the stick and said:

"Stick, please Stick, will you beat the dog?

Dog won't bite my pig,

Pig won't climb over the stile and I shan't get home in time for supper."

But the stick would not beat the dog.

So Dame Trot looked around for some more help and she saw a fire. She went up to the fire and said:

"Fire, please Fire, will you burn the stick?
Stick won't beat Dog,
Dog won't bite my pig,
Pig won't climb over the stile and I shan't get home in time for supper."

But the fire would not burn the stick.

So Dame Trot looked around for some more help and she saw some water. She went up to the water and said:

"Water, please Water, will you put out the fire?
Fire won't burn Stick,
Stick won't beat Dog ,
Dog won't bite my pig,
Pig won't climb over the stile and I shan't get home in time for supper."

But the water would not put out the fire.

So Dame Trot looked around for some more help and she saw a cow. She went up to the cow and said:

"Cow, please Cow, will you drink the water?

Water won't put out Fire,

Fire won't burn Stick,

Stick won't beat Dog,

Dog won't bite my pig,

Pig won't climb over the stile and I shan't get home in time for supper."

But the cow would not drink the water.

So Dame Trot looked around for some more help and she saw a butcher. She went up to the butcher and said:

"Butcher, please Butcher, will you kill the cow?
Cow won't drink Water,
Water won't put out Fire,
Fire won't burn Stick,
Stick won't beat Dog,
Dog won't bite my pig,
Pig won't climb over the stile and I shan't get home in time for supper."

But the butcher would not kill the cow.

So Dame Trot looked around for some more help and she saw a piece of rope. She went up to the rope and said:

"Rope, please Rope, will you tie up the butcher?

Butcher won't kill Cow,

Cow won't drink Water,

Water won't put out Fire,

Fire won't burn Stick,

Stick won't beat Dog

Dog won't bite my pig,

Pig won't climb over the stile and I shan't get home in time for supper."

But the rope would not tie up the butcher.

So Dame Trot looked around for some more help and she saw a rat. She went up to the rat and said:

"Rat, please Rat, will you chew the rope?

Rope won't tie up Butcher,

Butcher won't kill Cow,

Cow won't drink Water,

Water won't put out Fire,

Fire won't burn Stick,

Stick won't beat Dog,

Dog won't bite my pig,

Pig won't climb over the stile and I shan't get home in time for supper."

But the rat would not chew the rope.

So Dame Trot looked around for some more help and she saw a cat. She went up to the cat and said:

"Cat, please Cat, will you chase the rat?

Rat won't chew Rope,

Rope won't tie up Butcher,

Butcher won't kill Cow,

Cow won't drink Water,

Water won't put out Fire,

Fire won't burn Stick,

Stick won't beat Dog,

Dog won't bite my pig,

Pig won't climb over the stile and I shan't get home in time for supper."

The cat looked at Dame Trot. It yawned and stretched itself out on the warm paving stones. It cleaned itself carefully all over with its tongue. Then it spoke:

"I am very thirsty. Find me a large saucerful of milk to drink, then I will do as you wish."

So Dame Trot found some milk and poured out a large saucerful and gave it to the cat. The cat drank it up all in one go. And as soon as the cat had drunk up all the milk......

The cat began to chase the rat,
the rat began to chew the rope,
the rope began to tie up the butcher,
the butcher began to kill the cow,
the cow began to drink the water,
the water began to put out the fire,
the fire began to burn the stick,
the stick began to beat the dog,
the dog began to bite the pig,
the pig climbed right over the stile........
and Dame Trot did get home in time for supper
after all!